WHERE HAVE ALL THE HORSES GONE?

WHERE HAVE ALL THE HORSES GONE?

BY BILL WESTBROOK AND THOMAS HALE

STORY CONCEPT,
DESIGN AND
ILLUSTRATIONS
BY THOMAS HALE

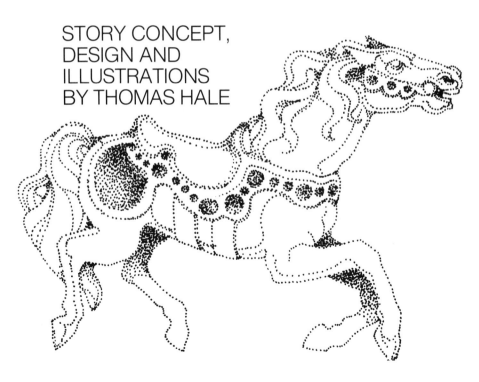

Westover
Publishing Company
A Media General Publication   Richmond, Virginia

To our sons.
Don't ever grow up no matter
what anybody says.

unlight was slowly, quietly dyeing the darkness a pale yellow.

Wrapped only in the cold winter air he felt brittle, as though if you touched a leg it would simply crack and fall off. Which it might have done in his condition. But anyway, he didn't want to be touched at all. He wasn't just cold outside. He was cold inside too.

He looked down at the ground. He was getting a shadow. A prancing black shadow pushing slowly out into the dirt aisle.

You couldn't tell anything about him except his shape from the shadow. Stretching, trying to run yet frozen in the morning. Or was he trying?

His silhouette was probably his most handsome feature now. But when he was young and just getting started, well, he could remember he was something. They were all something.

He was aware of birth but he couldn't feel it.

First, someone had to cut the whitewood for his body. Only whitewood would do. Then the wood was cut into thick planks and put together to form a large square block, hollow on the inside.

Someone else cut into the block with a carving machine and gave him the rough beginnings of a body.

Someone carved his legs but left them, like a prancing amputee's limbs, in a pile in the corner of the shop for awhile. They pawed the air silently.

Someone gave him a tail carved like it was in a hurricane and fitted it to his rump.

And then someone, a master carver, put him all

2

together and made him whole. The carver finished his body by hand, sculpting his saddle from the whitewood. He gave it straps inset with bright jewels, and a rolled and tufted blanket with an Indian design.

The carver's calloused hands stroked the square block that would be his head and pushed a cold steel bit into it. Gently, he pushed with his hands and tapped with his wooden mallet. Gouging, smoothing, gouging deeper, the whitewood falling like orange peels at his feet.

The block of wood sensed but he could not feel. The smell of his own body filled his nostrils.

The carver labored over the expression, spreading the lips wide and curling them back to bare his teeth. Hung his tongue over the bit and out the side of his gaping mouth.

The carver laid his ears back and under a beating mane. Into waiting white sockets the carver placed bright black jewels.

His wooden look was fierce and straining at first glance, but his eyes were only mischievous, as if it were all a bluff.

His legs were found in the corner and fitted, and he galloped at a standstill, a finished carving. White. Nude. Like a Christmas tree waiting for lights and ornaments.

Then, to the paint room. First, a gleaming white undercoat that filled his nicks and soaked into his cracks, dripping off the tips of his ears onto his neck, running silent races down his chest and legs to quarter-sized puddles sprinkled beneath him.

The enamel brushed smoothly onto his saddle, a shiny black. Reins and straps were painted a bright red with silver fittings and buckles. His teeth were gleaming white; the inside of his mouth pink like the in-side of everyone's mouth.

And his body, which could have been black or brown or white or roan or spotted or even striped was painted, instead, a dapple gray. A smooth, gray hide with cloudy, rounded patches of white on his rump and chest.

Lastly, small brass horseshoes were tacked to his flying hoofs. New and gleaming, they caught the light and bounced it off the walls and the underside of his belly. As he stood there right out of the oven, those brass shoes clicked in his imagination against cobble-stones and sent sparks flying. His muscles bulged in his shoulders as he flew. The skin barely stretched to wrap his powerful hind legs and his tendons ran like taut clotheslines to his hoofs. Foam oozed under his breast plate as it chafed his powerful chest. Saliva was sent flinging off his tongue against the wind and back past the rider crouched low in the blackness of the saddle and night, grasping the jeweled horn in one hand, the jerking leather reins in the other.

He was quite easily the most majestic carousel horse the factory had ever produced. The carvers said it every time.

Of course, his right side was his best side. That was the only side, for instance, that had jewels in the straps and in the saddle. It was the only side, too, that had detailed carving of the muscles and Indian blanket and saddle. The left side of his body was just nowhere.

It bothered him a little, this right side-left side business. It seemed a little dishonest because the right side was the side all the people would see while they were waiting to ride the carousel. That's what they'd think they were getting for their money. Of course, they might not ever notice the difference. But even if the people didn't know, there was still the fact that he did.

> I mean, it's my body, he thought. Everywhere I go, I go like this. With this plain birthmark over half of me. People think I'm one thing, but I'm only half that. There's another side they'll probably never see.

Around him in the storeroom of the carousel factory there were lions, tigers, pigs, ostriches, giraffes and lots of other horses. All just as one-sided as he. There were also two chariots; big, gold leaf chariots

5

emblazoned with eagles and scroll work. Two white chariot horses with carved gold plumes and red roses along their saddle lines and saddle straps stood at the ready in front of each chariot.

Other horses stood everywhere like photographs, caught dead in their poses. Waiting. Agonizingly straining to move, caught like children in a game of perpetual "red light."

Then, one morning, the waiting was over. The dapple gray carousel horse was packed in straw in a big, wooden crate and loaded onto a train. He couldn't tell how long he traveled. In the darkness there was no sound to hold onto, no sight to fix time or perspective. He had only himself in the blackness. Maybe the dapple gray was heartsick at leaving the carousel factory. Or maybe there was just not enough in him yet to make conversation with. But it was a lonely trip.

When the train finally stopped in its tracks, the dapple gray was unloaded onto a truck and driven through a town to a park with rolling green meadows and green trees rising here and there. Down the hill was a small pond where bright white ducks were swimming.

It was the first time the dapple gray had ever seen the world outside the carousel factory. And it was the first time he had ever seen real animals.

A little boy was feeding the ducks popcorn down at the pond. The ducks quacked and honked as they fought for the white prizes from the little boy's bag, each piece landing on the water with the smallest of splashes.

> *Now this is depressing,* thought the dapple gray. *I can't make a sound like real animals; I can't move when I want; I can't dash off through meadows; I can't eat grass; I can't drink water; I can't do one thing a real animal can do. That's just great. Of all the things I could be born as, I had to be born as an unreal animal.*

He watched the ducks swimming about the pond. He could hear the little boy giggling and laughing as he emptied his bag into the water and headed up the hill towards the emptying trucks.

The dapple gray felt overwhelmed by the circumstances of his birth. He tried to lift his legs and run, tried with all his strength and willpower, but his hard, bright muscles never twitched. He tried to whinny, tried to blow the air out of his mouth to show he was alive and needed someone to know it, but not a breath came. He only stood in his straw, leaning against the crate, looking out from behind glass eyes.

The little boy climbed and raced to the top of the hill to the excitement of his first carousel. Men in gray overalls and bright red and black check shirts were un-loading the huge brown platform from a flatbed trailer. Some other men were swinging the huge carousel engine into place with a yellow crane that looked like a praying mantis on its hind legs, twisting about, up and down.

Bright yellow straw was about, very clean under the animals.

The little boy walked through the carousel's parts, bug-eyed and completely overpowered by the excitement. The dapple gray watched as he hopped out of the way of the workmen and made his way to the animals.

He stopped to get into one of the chariots, picked up the reins and called out to his chargers. None of the workmen seemed to mind as he laughed and played.

But the strangest thing was happening inside the dapple gray as he watched. The strangest kind of sensation down deep within his hollowness. He heard the giggles and saw the delight of the little boy and the smallest kind of a feeling ached in him.

He watched the boy climb from the chariot and run from animal to animal, at once climbing onto the pig's broad back and then wiggling under the giraffe's legs, in turn petting and stroking each one.

And then the boy spotted the dapple gray. And the little horse saw the look in the boy's eyes, the same look he had seen go to the chariot and the pig and the other animals, that look now came to him.

It came to him as the boy did, stroking and patting his neck, rubbing his forehead and scratching behind his ears. The little fingers brushed his mane and, moving down his chest to his prancing hoofs, tapped the brass horseshoes as if checking for stones. Then the boy pushed his foot into the stirrup and was up on his back in a flash.

Together they charged the daylight, swooped to the tops of hills, through shallow creeks with water splashing over the two of them, down the sides of mountains, along beaches and across hot deserts, into rain forests and up snowbanks; they drank from icy winter lakes and camped by a thousand campfires. The boy and his horse kicked their heels at every danger, outran every enemy; through dusty towns they rode, through brush fires and wind storms, though hungry and exhausted half the time, they clung to each other, never deserted each other, for after all they had been through together, all the adventures of a moment, theirs was an immediate and special friendship.

There's nothing unreal about this,
the dapple gray thought. *I'm real. My
wood is real wood and my eyes are
real glass and my horseshoes are
real brass. So are those ducks down
at the pond any more real than I am?*

9

He decided of course not. Being real or not real was just something somebody made up about you. And if somebody had special feelings about you, those were real enough feelings, and they made you real.

Since it was getting dark, the men were covering the animals with tarps for the night, putting their tools away and closing their trucks.

The little boy slid from the saddle, gave the dapple gray one last hug, and ran home through the night. But sometime before the boy left, the little ache in the dapple gray's body had left. And he did not seem as hollow as before.

The next morning it seemed like all the town's children discovered the carousel going up in the park. They swarmed like ants to a piece of cheese, over it and through it. The workmen sometimes stopped to scold them but the children never seemed to hear.

A thin, red-headed man dressed in khaki work clothes gave orders to the workmen about where to put what. He walked in and out of the animals, looking, running his eyes over their lines. He came to the ostrich and the giraffe and he walked around and around. He squinted one eye like an artist at the chariots, and smiled. To each animal he gave a nodding approval.

The dapple gray watched as he approached him, studied him as he had the other animals. The man's face was tight, but generous at the mouth and his eyes squinted at the corners. His skin was a deep tan and he held an unlit, beat-up pipe in his hand, which he was now pointing in the dapple gray's direction as he talked with one of the workmen.

"Let's put this gray on the outside," he said. "And then let's get those two white horses out of the truck along with that black jumper and put them inside this gray in one row."

With that he walked off with the workman. The thin, red-headed man with the unlit pipe was in charge of the carousel, it seemed to the dapple gray. At least, he was putting it together the way he wanted it.

Soon the dapple gray was lifted into position on the outside of the platform and his long brass pole was pushed through him. It made him feel very strong and sure of himself.

I know who I am, he thought. *I know where I'm going. I've got my place right here on this pole. If I get scared I can just squeeze my sides together and hold on that much tighter.*

By that night, all the animals were in place on their poles. All the bright light bulbs had been screwed in. The band organ had been tuned up for the carousel's opening in the morning.

Down below the hill in the town, little lights twinkled and slowly, blinked off. The children were nervously trying to get to sleep while riding carousel horses in their heads.

At the carousel, the animals waited in the dark for morning.

Eyes open, as always, the dapple gray looked into the blackness and listened. He wasn't afraid of this night. The pole held him tightly to the carousel and he could sense, if he could not quite see, the other animals around him.

Suddenly a small vibration went through his pole. Then another. Footsteps on the platform. There were feet moving on the other side that he could feel and hear, but could not see.

In a slow, halting walk the footsteps came closer. Around the circle by the chariots, past the red donkey and the ostrich running at a standstill. A form showed itself in the dim moonlight, flashed an impression in an instant to the glass eyes wide open in the darkness. A thin figure.

Through the smells of the night, a fragrance of burning tobacco reached the dapple gray's nostrils. Reached him as a hand landed softly on his rump.

If he could have started and jumped he surely would have. But the hand was friendly as it patted him. It belonged to the carousel man.

The man hummed to himself softly as he left the little horse's side and walked down the row, past the two white horses and the jumping black to the band organ. He fumbled around in the dark behind the organ for a moment, and in an instant the lights of the carousel were on brightly. Brilliant in the night's blackness, the colored lights bounced off the glazed bodies beneath them.

Another moment, and the carousel was moving. The music was playing. The animals were going up and down and around to the accompaniment of the band organ. And there was the carousel man standing in the center of his world as it spun around him, just getting the feel of it.

So this is the carousel, thought the dapple gray. *Don't stop. Don't ever stop going around. I never want to get off.*

The dapple gray saw the other animals in bright lights for the first time. Movement made them wholly different.

The big, fat blue and white pigs with red saddles and shiny silver stirrups had to strain to run. Their short, squat legs seemed to ripple under the pounds of their bodies as the carousel lights whirled by.

There were elf-like black mice scampering around with bursting eyes and gray collars and gray reins.

13

And the baby elephants. White and green and purple all in a row. Heaving forward, massive; you could imagine their trumpeting, trampling through rain forests.

There were tigers and lions, bright gold with orange saddles and blankets, lunging forward, teeth bared, clawing the bright electric air.

The band organ tooted the night with its high pitched melody. Oom-pah-pah, oom-pah-pah, oom-pah-pah-pah.

Behind the carousel man, in the engine well, the big black engine clanked its own certain chorus. With grease in its guts and gears with shiny teeth and black gums, the big engine turned the groaning wooden carousel around and around.

The carousel man laughed with the excitement. He hopped from animal to animal, climbed to their backs and rode each a full circle or two. He found the dapple gray and rode him around and around, laughing and humming oom-pah-pah-pah to the music going out into the night.

The dapple gray wished the man would never get off. It was the feeling he'd had with the boy who'd first gotten on him. He felt special tonight. Special, because the carousel man wanted to be alone with his carousel before the rest of the world had it for their toy.

They went on like that, the carousel man and his animals, until he had ridden every one. And when he had ridden every one he shut off the engine, cut off the lights and left the carousel as quiet as it had ever been.

The next morning, which was opening day at the carousel, it rained. Just like it rains on a thousand opening days everywhere.

It began raining lightly just before dawn. The dapple gray, who had never experienced rain, was somewhat bewildered by it at first. It rolled under the canopy in big balls of mist and coated him with tiny drops, almost like perspiration. It dripped off the canopy down to the ground and made a little ring of holes all around the carousel.

But in the mist and in the mud, with their umbrellas and their slickers and rubbers, with bright eyes and wet fuzzy cheeks the children came. In long lines they waited, umbrellas bumping clumsily into each other like so many colored mushrooms in a strong wind, their bases teetering. And one by one the carousel man took their tickets, started his wonderful machine and sent them into heaven.

They lived there all summer. The children came, paid their dimes to the carousel man and they didn't care if they ever got off. There was magic in the music and the music was in their ears.

Oh sure, at home there were toys to wind up or swings to swing. But there was nothing with the movement and the sound and the power to take you away like a carousel. Just be on a carousel horse and the adventures would crowd on top of one another.

The boys would all be cowboys. Or, sometimes, knights in shining armor. The girls would always be circus queens; they'd practice their tricks in short, fluffy costumes as their bare thighs squeaked against the shiny wooden saddles in the warm summer air.

With every ride the dapple gray kicked his heels in the air and flew. What the children saw in him, he was beginning to see in himself. Whether or not he was wooden or flesh, or had a heart or a knothole in his chest didn't matter. When he shared something special with children, each jewel in his saddle shone like a different sunset on a different trail. His colors were rainbows after showers in the mountains. He was something to see, and he liked it.

One morning when the carousel man spent an unusual amount of time dusting and shining the carousel, the dapple gray got especially excited. The carousel man polished the brass poles and the chariots; he shined the rooster and the giraffe and the elephants and all the horses; he swept the platform clean of dirt and paper and cups; he greased the carousel engine and oiled the big, booming band organ.

He's getting ready for the mayor's kids, thought the dapple gray. *I never looked like this when I was new.*

He didn't know, though, that the carousel man had put a sign at the gate entrance that said the carousel would be closed until noon.

It was 10:30 when a bus pulled up at the gate with the reason. There on the side, in black letters just below the row of 14 windows, was a sign: SCHOOL FOR THE BLIND.

Up the hill, up the concrete white sidewalk tapped 22 blind children with their thin red and white sticks.

The dapple gray watched them huddle together in the warm morning air with their teacher, standing in front of the carousel man who was standing so proudly in front of his shiny machine. Strangely, the dapple gray felt nervous.

The teacher talked with the carousel man for a few minutes, then they helped the children step up to the platform. Small vibrations throbbed through the carousel as the children tapped their sticks before them, finding their way between the rows of animals.

A dark little boy with a red and white and brown striped shirt tapped his way to where the dapple gray rested at the end of his last gallop. They stood nose to nose; each was as afraid as the other.

17

Slowly the boy's hands reached for the dapple gray, felt his wooden face, found the small cracks and steel bit marks that had almost been lost under the paint. His little hands could almost fit into the horse's nostrils. Into his mouth they went, feeling his tongue and teeth and metal bit. Up his face, his long hard face, tracing his bridle to his ears. He found his eyes with one hand, and the dapple gray did not blink when he gently followed the contours of his eyelids with his fingers. The boy was reading his face, sensing his expression.

Down the dapple gray's body he went. Down by the side where there were no jewels to shine or colors to make rainbows after mountain showers. Down the side that no one was supposed to see.

The dapple gray felt naked, turned inside out by someone who could not see him.

Slowly the small hands outlined the dapple gray and finally, in a moment, the boy's thin arms flew around the horse's neck. His cane fell to the platform with a final tap. He jumped and climbed his way onto the dapple gray's back, grasped the neck of his mind's horse, and rode with him the very longest time the carousel man had ever let the carousel run at a stretch.

And they had their adventures, galloping to distant places the dapple gray had never visited. The horse felt the sun on his back, really felt it, for the first time. And with the boy, he heard the sweetest carousel music he had ever heard.

When it ended, as the ride must always end, the boy didn't want to get off. He clasped his little hands tightly under his horse's neck and cried silently. And on his neck the dapple gray felt the warm wetness of tears, like a mountain shower the two of them shared. Drops ran into him through invisible cracks and fell, one by one, into a puddle inside him.

But if there was any puddle left inside him now, it had long since turned to ice.

The dapple gray had changed a lot in twenty-three years. Age had made his paint flake like a moulting skin. And in places his paint was blistered, his whitewood blackened with soot. A thin, hairline crack ran from one shoulder down a foreleg, widened and traveled to his hoof to split open at the end like a tributary emptying into a river. His jewels were dull and dirty, and several had dropped off and left pockmark scars. His ears were cracked and the tip of one had been snapped off at some time. Even his once shiny brass horseshoes were tarnished.

He was just beaten and broken after years of rides and, lately, rainy days out under the sky.

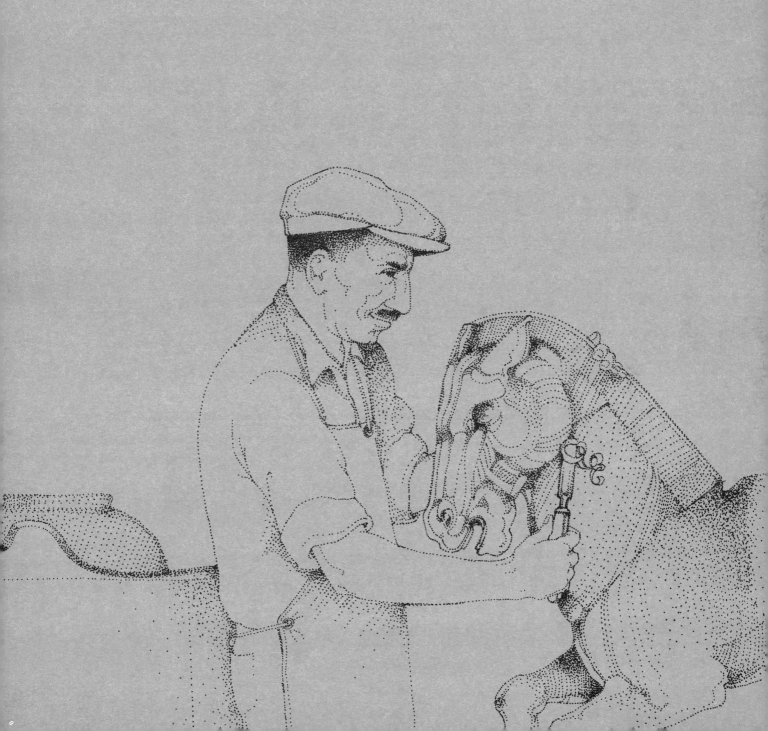

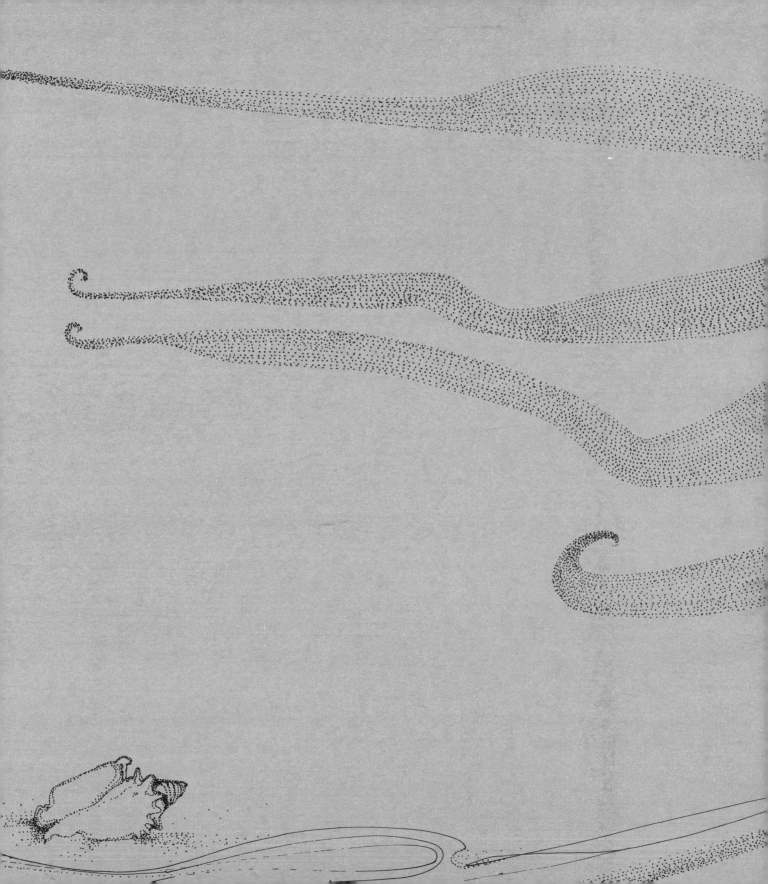

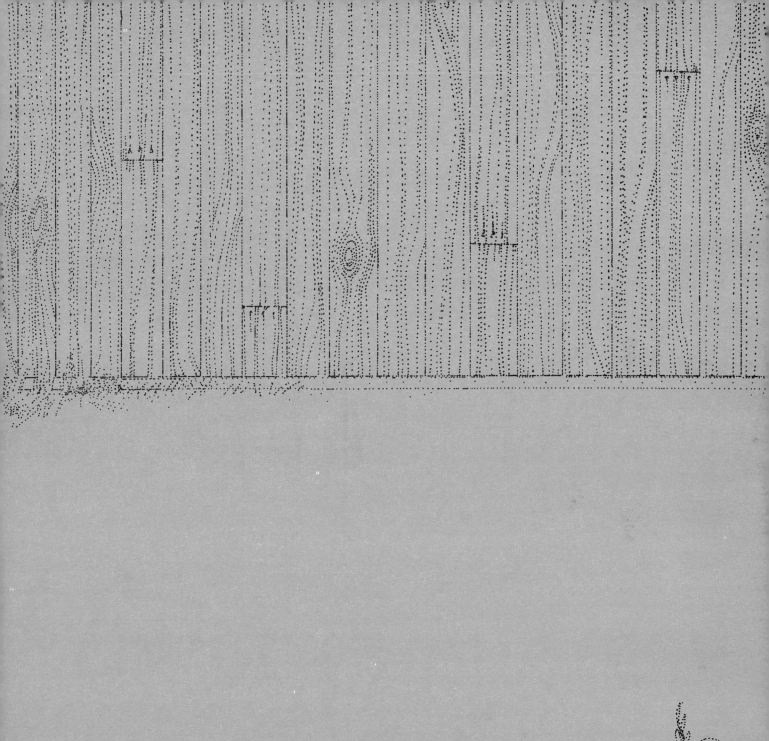

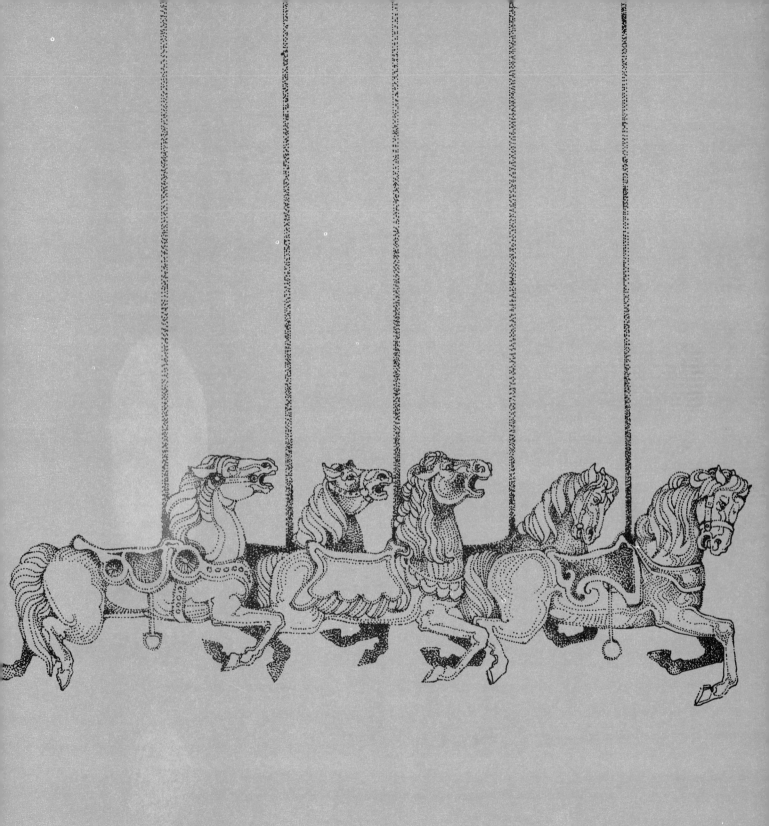

Life was no longer round and round, up and down, oom-pah- pah-pah.

The row of proud stallions that once had leaped in front of him were gone. And around him, where the children had always been, lay scattered the junked bits and pieces of unimportant matter. It was as if the dapple gray was at the bottom of a big garbage can filled with everything second-hand. Twisted metal pipes, fat wooden barrels with splitting sides, bicycle wheels turning quietly to rust, tires that couldn't get air, buckets that couldn't hold water, broken baby dolls shivering without clothes in the cold afternoon air, all the small pieces of yesterday that life had used up and then collected in the junkyard to be trophies for infrequent hunters.

Since he couldn't shut his eyes to make the place go away, he went back into his life on long trips in his mind.

I can't keep going on like this, he thought. *You can't just ignore right here and now. But it's just that thinking back makes me young again inside. It doesn't get me anywhere. But then, I'm not getting anywhere as it is.*

His only visitor in a long while had been a little black spider that had quietly strung its silver wires from one stirrup to a foreleg. Swinging, letting the strands out slowly, the spider had worked all morning without stopping to rest.

> *Well, I might as well be useful for something. Something is better than nothing,* thought the dapple gray.

Still, he'd never had a spider web on him in his life. The carousel man had seen to that, all right. The dapple gray wished his rag was going over him now, polishing, shining, the way it had, well, even the last time they were together before the trouble started.

It was the children, actually, who gave the dapple gray the first hint that something was wrong. The children would ride the carousel longer, would ride it well into dark, if the carousel man would let them. And lately, he had let them a lot.

Something was coming, the dapple gray knew it. From down below the hill and off in the distance, he could hear the sound of Caterpillars inching their way towards him. He could smell the burning black tar when the wind carried it to him. And he could see black dots in the sky from the smoking engines.

What was coming was The Road. It was winding, snaking its way around buildings, looking for a strip of land wide enough to eat up. The carousel park was in its mouth.

There was no saving the carousel from The Road. The carousel was old and needed too many repairs. The engine was out of gas. The platform was rotting away. The roof leaked. There were a thousand reasons.

It just seemed like the best thing to do was sell as many of the carousel's parts as possible and junk the rest. It was no use. The people were infected with the idea of growth and prosperity. And that kind of infection, once it gets in a town, is incurable.

The dapple gray did not go around as usual that summer. He went around trying to understand what they were doing to him.

I suppose you have to stop riding the carousel sometime, he thought. *But why, just because you grow older. It seems so automatic. One year you ride. The next year you're too old to ride. People who ride Caterpillars never ride carousel horses. That's the problem.*

Toward the last of the summer a feeler came from a traveling outfit called The Goodtime Show & Carnival. The word was that the carnival man would come look at the carousel within a week.

The dapple gray didn't like what he felt inside of him. And for the first time, he didn't like the carousel man fussing over him, polishing and shining. He knew the carousel man wasn't enjoying it.

The carnival man from The Goodtime Show & Carnival showed up that next week as he'd promised. And by the way he fine-tooth-combed the carousel, the dapple gray began to sense what he'd come for. The little horse watched him as the carousel went around.

"Well, you've done pretty good by these animals, sir," he told the carousel man.

The carnival man's face was round and brown, and he smiled from inside a suit that was wrinkled on its back and behind its knees.

"Of course, I don't know what I can take, you see. Maybe a spare animal here and there in case any of mine should ever wear out."

He was missing a heel off one shoe.

"Come to think of it, I've got a couple of horses wore out right now."

He wiped his brow with a spotted handkerchief and put it back, almost all the way, into his pocket.

"Kids wear out a horse in no time these days, don't you know. Wear me out, too. Sometimes I think I'll just get out of this business so I don't have them

41

yelling kids to listen to all the time, you know?"

The carousel man didn't know. He didn't know anything except this round-faced man in front of him came to buy part of him that he didn't want to sell.

The carnival man went on and the carousel went around. And when the deal was finally over he'd bought 25 animals. The dapple gray had been almost the last to go.

No judge of horseflesh, thought the dapple gray.

But it wasn't funny like he wanted it to be.

The surprise was that the carnival man had brought his own workmen to take the animals back with him that day. They worked fast. By noon they had the horses lying in the grass like slaughtered animals. The carnival man circled them, moved around them as the sun gleamed off their bodies.

Suddenly he paused in his circling, as if to question the carousel man about his good deal, and asked, "Tell me, why are they selling the carousel?"

The dapple gray lay on his side, one eye looking up into the deep, blue air. Birds flew in and out of his vision. A few ants had started exploring his body to find out what had intruded on their grass.

Why are they selling the carousel?
he thought. *Why are they? It's not
The Road. That's just something to
point to. It's not the repairs. Sure,
they'd be expensive, but they've always been made before. What then?*

The carousel man sat on the edge of his platform, looking down. Slowly he raised his eyes and
stared for a moment at his horses in the grass. In the
back of his mind he heard carousel music. He heard
children laughing and running for their favorite horses.
He heard the flick of a light switch, good night.

"They're selling the carousel," he said, "because they're not old enough to want to remember riding it. You only need these kinds of things when you're
very young or very old."

The carousel man and the carnival man just
looked at each other through the daylight. Looked the
way people do when there's nothing more to say.
Beyond that moment, or beyond that hill or that park,
they seemed as out of place as their animals. Just two
old anachronisms caught in front of a new road coming
over top of them.

As he was being carried to the waiting truck, the
dapple gray looked one last time at the carousel behind
him. It seemed as if some giant monster had taken a
big bite off of it, like a cookie. Or as if someone had

43

come in broad daylight, the great carousel thief, and stolen part of it right in front of the town's eyes. The carousel was crippled; its music would never play again.

As for the carousel man, well, 23 years is a lot to say goodbye to. Maybe too much, because he didn't stay around long. He just made a sign for the gate that read: CAROUSEL PARK CLOSED. For the first time, he didn't say what time it would reopen.

Meanwhile, the dapple gray was riding in the blanket blackness of the truck and wondering where he was going. He bumped with cushioned knocks into the animals on either side of him, and waited.

It was two days before the carnival man caught up with his Goodtime Show. They found it on a bright morning as it was busy setting up just outside a small town.

Workmen unloaded the animals at the far end of the midway where a silent carousel stood waiting.

Once again, the horses were laid in the grass. The animals on the carousel looked silently down at their replacements. The dapple gray felt uneasy under their gaze. Vulnerable. But he made himself return their stares. Made himself participate in this cold war. For a moment, his mind must have wandered; he dreamed he was on the carousel looking down.

He was staring at the carousel for several moments like this before he started seeing it. It was barely alive. The animals were gasping for air and life. They were bruised and tortured from night after one-night stands and morning knockdowns. Crippled, they stood self-consciously without their bridles or reins, or with an ear missing or a foot almost in splinters. Their nicks and holes showed down to their white base paint; scratches ripped like pencil marks along their sides. Their poles were tarnished except where the children's hands had polished them. But, oddly, they were not bright even there.

One by one the old animals were taken down and the not-quite-as-old animals were fitted into place. It didn't take long on this kind of carousel. It was made to knock down and put back up in a hurry.

The dapple gray was put on the inside. Beneath him he could see where the oil stains from the engine well had outlined their shapes on the worn, brown floorboards. Overhead, the thin yellow awning rose and fell, puffing quietly in a new breeze.

The dapple gray looked out past a row of horses, out and down the midway to see what he'd come to. The striped canvas on the fronts of the exhibit tents and sideshows had long ago beat itself loudly on the windy plains of the midwest or on the sides of mountain towns. But now it hung faded, colorless, flap-

45

ping a dull, incessant beat without life in its threads.

In front of the tents, barred ticket booths, alone and empty. Their layers of blue and white paint split along their sides. The daylight wasn't kind to this Good-time Show. It revealed all its flaws and hurts.

But nighttime soon came, and the bright little colored lights came on and threw their small shadows over the nicks and scratches. The rides squeaked and groaned, jerked forward by hoarse, coughing engines. Barkers in their frayed, shabby costumes barked their come-on calls to handfuls of bystanders walking aimlessly by. It wasn't a big night.

The carousel horse went around and round on the inside track. It was a lot different when you were on the inside looking out. The world didn't go by as fast, for one thing. The music seemed to ring in his ears a little louder. The smell of oil and grease from the carousel engine was stronger.

And, too, this new carousel man was always nearby because he was always working on the engine. Grease was black on his arms and thick in the cracks of his hands. He had dirt and oil on his cheeks, rimming his mouth like a clown's face. And a cigarette was kept pursed between his lips, always with an ash hanging, bent and gray. To the dapple gray he seemed more like a mechanic than a carousel man. It was as if taking the children's tickets interrupted keeping his engine going.

No matter, really. The Goodtime Show's carousel went around that winter half full anyway. Every stop was the same. Bunches of people instead of crowds. And since there were few riders, there was no money to repair the rides. There was no applause for the performers, so the performers, one by one, left.

Afternoons were for set-up. Mornings were for knockdowns. The rides first. Then the side-show tents collapsed and, like the air rushing out of a balloon, they flattened and lay exhausted.

The dapple gray was becoming chipped and bruised from the knockdowns and he didn't look so special anymore. His pole squeaked when he galloped and called attention to him just when he wanted to disappear.

As for the children, well, they didn't treat him with such special favor anymore, either. Of course, he wasn't ridden as much as the outside jumpers, but when he was ridden there were no real adventures. The children didn't pay to stay on him and ride him into the night. They didn't stroke his peeling neck and cluck to him to go faster. They didn't scratch behind his ears where the cracks were widening. He was a one-night stand out of a whole year of nights. And one night, one boy had even put gum under his neck.

His pride, so long built up by care and affection, simply weakened and, eventually, left.

47

I can't understand it, he thought. *I can't understand gum under a carousel horse's neck. I hope none of the other animals see. And yet I wonder if something worse has happened to them. Maybe someone's carved initials into the fat pig's back. Or maybe someone's taken a jewel out of the giraffe's saddle. Why?*

It just killed him inside. His specialness just drained out of him until he was empty. There was no carousel man fussing over his horses to find gum under his neck. Or to ride him when the children didn't. Or even to oil his squeaking pole.

So the dapple gray was hollow again. A peeling wooden horse on his last go-round.

Slowly, the charm of the carousel wore off and, eventually, was lost. It became monotonous to him, this going round and round. Town after town and the music never changed. You went around once and then the view never changed.

It's just pointless to go around in circles all the time, the dapple gray thought. *All my life I've done that. I wonder why it's taken me so long to figure it out.*

Traveling was worse, though. Traveling meant being boxed up in the blackness for days at a time, suffocating in the breath of a truck full of animals. It meant knocks and jolts and dust blowing through floorboard cracks to coat your eyes and fill your mouth. It meant small, silent cries that the drivers never heard.

So the dapple gray was glad one night when the carnival man, after seeing a better than average turnout for two days, decided to stay over an extra night. But, as the Goodtime Show's luck would have it, towards evening it began raining heavily. The few people who were riding under the shelter of the canopy were quickly frightened away by the loud cracks of thunder followed in seconds by bright flashes of lightning.

Even the carousel's mechanic gave up his work on the engine and ran for the cover of his trailer. The animals remained alone to wait out the storm's battering. Even on the inside of the row the slashing rain found the dapple gray and sent a cold spray over him.

The carousel shook with the thunder and the canvas beat like a flag, popping and snapping. The bright flashes of lightning illuminated the whole carnival; it looked like a ghost town, with empty streets and deserted shops and stores.

The dapple gray stood frozen in position, the rain drops dripping from his face and hoofs and tail. Suddenly there was the loudest crack he had ever heard and the carousel seemed for an instant as if all its lights were on. And, then, blackness again.

But something was left behind. In the mist under the canopy, under sheets of water that beat down and threatened to drown the carousel, the tiniest silver-gray thread of smoke floated to the dapple gray's nostrils, filled them with fear and sent panic into his eyes.

Fire! His gaping mouth screamed it silently into the pellets of water dripping from his nose. Panic welled up inside him but he couldn't move. Above him, a small blaze hung under the canopy, eating it from the inside out. Smoke hung like fog in the air beside the animals until there was nothing to see but bright flashes through its grayness. Nothing to hear but spitting fire fighting the rain.

I've got to run! gasped the dapple gray. *I'll burn to death if I don't get off this pole. Someone see this! Someone! Get the animals off! Let me off!*

Sheets of canvas were flaming, burning overhead and dropping to the platform. The dapple gray struggled with all the fight he had left in his body, fought to force his wooden muscles to run, to bolt to the freedom of the rain outside.

But the pole he'd always held onto so tightly now held onto him. He felt like a prisoner, but he was just a carousel horse who couldn't change what he was. Besides, where could he run to on his own?

Canvas hung like curtains on either side of him, burning brightly. The oil pools around the engine were on fire, throwing an eerie light on him from below. On his rump and saddle the paint bubbled and burst; his belly was black from the oil's smoke and the tip of his tail glowed a bright orange.

I'm burning! I'm on fire! Can't any-one hear me? he yelled into the night. *The animals will all die if you don't stop this!*

By the time the carnival workers reached the carousel it was glowing like a bonfire. The dapple gray stood helplessly in the heat and smoke as the men fought the blazes around him.

Suddenly the muscles in his throat gripped him until his breath stopped in his chest as he saw a flaming carousel horse on the outside of his row slide slowly down its hot brass pole, dropping until it fell to the platform and split open like an ember falling through a grate, sending its last sparks spiraling upward.

Up into the night they went to mix with other sparks like crazy, zig-zagging stars whirling to dodge the rain drops.

Sometime later in the night the last spark was finally out. The weary carnival workmen sloshed back to their trailers to collapse. The carousel would never again suffer the bruised ribs of morning knockdowns.

Its pride would never hurt again from empty rides. It had burned in half that night; it was dead.

The dapple gray stood blackened with soot in the black night. The smell of wet ashes rose from the platform of the gutted carousel. Around him the grotesque remains of charred, burned and blackened animals. The giraffe, the pigs, the mice and many horses were gone.

For all his unhappiness on this carousel, the dapple gray stood, with blister sores all over his body from burns, and the drops ran from his eyes as rain water.

It was now late afternoon in the junkyard. The sun formed jagged shadows from the scraps of things around the dapple gray carousel horse.

Nearby, he could hear the muffled growl of big trucks along the highway carrying their cargoes, keeping their rendezvous with far-away towns.

The dapple gray did not like to remember his truck rides. They had all been bad, but of course they were all over now. The last one had brought him to the junkyard after they had auctioned off what was left of the carousel after the fire. What else it had brought, he didn't know.

I wonder if I'm the only carousel horse here, he thought. *I can't see any more. You end up like this and you wonder how everybody else ended up. Where have all the horses gone? I mean, are there always fires that destroy carousels?*

Out in front of him from somewhere across the junkyard he could hear the mumbling of two voices. Then trucks went by outside again and he could not hear them anymore.

The spider web across his side from his stirrup to his foreleg was almost complete, and the sun acknowledged its presence with the slightest kind of a shadow underneath.

Now the dapple gray heard a noise that sounded like footsteps. He strained to look to his sides, but he could see nothing down either aisle. But they were footsteps, and they were growing louder.

Suddenly a shadow leaped down the aisle, stretched out its long form so fast it frightened the dapple gray. At the end of the aisle, his back to the sun, a man stood looking down the row. The dapple gray squinted into the sun to see him.

Two children ran around the corner and stood beside the man holding his legs and hands. Together they walked down the aisle towards the dapple gray,

53

browsing. The man pushed his hands deeply into the pockets of his coat as he stopped and started, looking at all the pieces of things that used to be whole. The children left his side to play tag down a side aisle.

Inside the dapple gray a feeling was struggling to get free. A feeling that should have died long ago came through him, started down deep within him and rose to his eyes to brighten their glass. It was life.

I don't want to die here, he screamed in silence. *See me. Find me here. Get me now.*

The man walked closer, stopping to look at a broken doll a few yards away. The laughter of his children was off somewhere in the distance.

Come find me now, pleaded the dapple gray. *I'm here resting, just tired. I can still go with you.*

The man moved up the aisle and his eyes caught the dapple gray's. The dapple gray fought to hold his stare. Fought to pull him to his side the way he might have twenty years before.

The man walked to him and stood looking down. The dapple gray tried to squeeze his cracks closed under the man's gaze. Tried to force spirit into his lines. Tried to flex his tired muscles and make them hard again.

They stood looking at each other through the late afternoon winter air.

> *Remember we rode in the mountains?* asked the dapple gray desperately. *Remember we pounded along beaches in the summer and up into the hills to camp? I always came when you called. See me now. Find me back in your mind.*

The man whistled softly to himself under his steaming breath. He looked at the dapple gray as if trying to remember the name of an old friend whose face he recognized. His eyes squinted and for a moment, the dapple gray thought he had finally seen him. But he thrust his hands deeper into the warmth of his pockets, turned and walked away.

The dapple gray's cracks opened up. His paint looked chipped again and his eyes cloudy. His muscles felt like sponges heavy with the water of afternoon rains. The spirit in his lines was broken.

He watched silently as the man walked away. The thought came to him that the rides were really over. The music wasn't going to play for him again. The man walking away from him down the aisle wasn't going to look back.

The sun was going down over the back of the junkyard as the giggles of a children's game floated over the piles of scrap. But the dapple gray didn't seem to notice. His eyes were trying to close and his ears were growing deaf.

The two children flew around the corner at the far end of the aisle. In the distance their father walked, separated from his children by more than the space of years between their ages. And yet they raced to catch up with him, the air steaming out of their mouths and nostrils as their arms pumped at their sides. Far away they looked small. But the closer they came, the bigger and older they seemed.

Suddenly, as they flew past, something caught their eyes. Something clicked in their minds in an instant and held them still in their youth. Something caught them in their race and suspended time while they went to faraway places they'd never seen before. Something fired their imagination and erased all the coldness from their bodies and held them fixed upon a broken carousel horse jutting out from a heap of useless junk.

There, on the side above a spider's silver web, two jewels on a saddle glowed like sunsets at the end of different trails. Brilliant colors bowed over the children and the horse like a rainbow and captured them, each the other's willing prisoner.

The jewels burned into the dapple gray's side like hot coals. Timidly, he felt his power return. Felt his magic draw small hands to him that could not feel wide cracks or broken bones. Eyes that could not see broken dreams in his eyes. Feet that effortlessly popped the strands of a spider's web to set him free.

A last spark of sunlight flickered in his eyes. With all his strength he tried to rear his head, struggled to tighten his muscles and arch his neck to strike a charger's pose, fought in his own wooden way to be all that he could be to two children who believed in him.

For the dapple gray carousel horse, maybe the rides weren't over. Perhaps the carousel had just stopped a while to change riders. And now, when everyone was on, they could begin again.

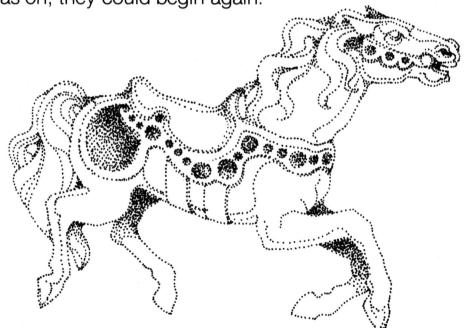